We're Busy, Charlie Brown!

Peanuts® characters created and drawn by Charles M. Schulz

Text by Diane Namm
Background illustrations by Art and Kim Ellis

A GOLDEN BOOK • NEW YORK
Western Publishing Company, Inc., Racine, Wisconsin 53404

Copyright © 1988 United Feature Syndicate, Inc. All rights reserved. Printed in the U.S.A. by Western Publishing Company, Inc. No part of this book may be reproduced or copied in any form without written permission from the publisher. GOLDEN®, GOLDEN & DESIGN®, A GOLDEN BOOK®, and A GOLDEN TELL-A-TALE® BOOK are trademarks of Western Publishing Company, Inc. Library of Congress Catalog Card Number: 87-82328
ISBN: 0-307-07056-5   B C D E F G H I J K L M

It was Saturday, and Charlie Brown had nothing to do.

"I feel like playing," he said, stepping
outside. "I think I'll find Snoopy. Oh, Snoopy,
where are you?" Charlie Brown called as he
walked along.

Snoopy was busy fishing, and he had only one pole. He also made it clear that he would rather fish alone.

So off went Charlie Brown to look for someone else to play with.

Then Charlie Brown met Lucy. "Say, Lucy, do you want to play?" he asked.

"Forget it, Charlie Brown. I'm not in the mood today. Can't you see I'm sulking? Just go away!" said Lucy.

Next Charlie Brown went to Schroeder's house. He sat down and asked Schroeder if he would like to play.

"I'm busy playing the piano, Charlie Brown." That's all Schroeder would say.

"I guess I'll go find Linus, then," said
Charlie Brown, and he got up and walked
away to Linus' house.

"Hey, Linus. How about a game of catch?"
Charlie Brown asked.

"I'm sorry, Charlie Brown. I'm reading this great new book, and I just can't put it down," replied Linus.

Charlie Brown left him alone.

"Gee, I wish I could think of a really great game—a game that everyone would want to play," Charlie Brown said with a sigh.

Then Charlie Brown walked home alone,
thinking hard the whole way.

"I suppose I could ask my sister, Sally, to play," thought Charlie Brown unhappily. And so he did.

"No way, big brother, I'm busy today.
People to talk to—phone calls to answer,"
said Sally as the phone began to ring.

"Hey, big brother," called Sally. "This phone call is for you!"

"For me?" asked Charlie Brown. "I wonder who it could be?"

"Hi there, Chuck. It's Peppermint Patty.
Remember me?" she asked.

"Oh, gee," groaned Charlie Brown. "Just
who I don't want to talk to."

"What's that, Chuck? Are you there? Can you hear me? Guess what? Baseball season starts next week," Peppermint Patty said. "So it's time to start practice today!"

"Baseball practice! Yippee! Hurray! Now everyone will want to play!" Charlie Brown shouted happily.

Charlie Brown called Schroeder and said, "Round up the gang. It's time for baseball practice!"

Charlie Brown rushed to the baseball field.
He waited for his friends to arrive.

First came Lucy. Then Snoopy. Then
Peppermint Patty and Sally. Bringing up the
rear was Linus. And Schroeder came, too,
carrying his piano.

"Okay, guys, it's a new season," shouted
Charlie Brown.

Then he wound up to throw the first pitch
of the year.

Thwack! Linus hit the ball right out of the park!

"And I just know this season is gonna be our best," added Charlie Brown. He was happy at last to have his friends playing by his side.